Library of Congress Control Number: 2012935527

ISBN 978-0-545-20888-8 (hardcover)
ISBN 978-0-545-20889-5 (paperback)

12 13 14 15 16 17 18 19 20      16 17 18 19

Printed in Malaysia   108
First edition, September 2012
Edited by Cassandra Pelham
Book design by Kazu Kibuishi and Phil Falco
Creative Director: David Saylor

# AMULET

### KAZU KIBUISHI

## BOOK FIVE
## PRINCE OF THE ELVES

AN IMPRINT OF

**SCHOLASTIC**

YOU'VE NEVER HEARD ABOUT THE GREAT ERLKING?

THE STORIES ABOUT HIM ARE SO AMAZING.

HERE WE GO.

MY DAD DOESN'T LET ME READ STUFF LIKE THAT.

HE SAYS I NEED TO STAY FOCUSED ON SCHOOL.

HE DOESN'T WANT ME READING ANYTHING OTHER THAN OUR TRAINING MANUALS.

BUT I LEARN SO MUCH WHEN I READ STORIES.

THE BEST ONES ARE USUALLY TRYING TO TEACH US SOMETHING.

THAT'S WHAT HE'S AFRAID OF.

HE'S SCARED I WON'T TURN OUT LIKE HIM.

I'M SURE HE JUST WANTS WHAT'S BEST FOR YOU.

YOU DON'T KNOW MY DAD.

HE WANTS WHAT'S BEST--

--FOR EVERYONE ELSE.

I TAKE IT MAX PERFORMED WELL DURING HIS TESTS.

HE PASSED WITH FLYING COLORS.

MAX AND VIGO ARE THE BEST IN THEIR CLASS, BY A WIDE MARGIN.

PAT

ROY, I HOPE YOU'LL CONSIDER LETTING MAX SERVE ON THE GUARDIAN COUNCIL.

I DON'T OFTEN SEE YOUNG STONEKEEPERS WITH HIS LEVEL OF SKILL.

I'M HAPPY FOR YOU, MAX.

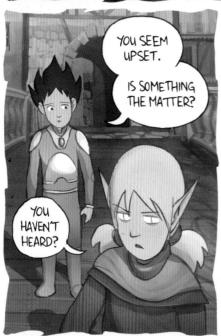

YOU SEEM UPSET.

IS SOMETHING THE MATTER?

YOU HAVEN'T HEARD?

MY PARENTS WERE TAKEN BY THE GUARD THIS MORNING.

LOOKS LIKE A WAR IS ABOUT TO BEGIN.

BUT YOUR FAMILY DIDN'T DO ANYTHING!

THIS HAS TO BE A MISTAKE!

I THINK IT'S BETTER IF YOU DON'T COME TO SEE ME, MAX.

FOR BOTH OUR SAKES.

MOM! DAD!

I WON'T LET THEM SEPARATE US AGAIN.

I ARRANGED FOR AN AIRSHIP TO TAKE YOU TO FRONTERA.

FROM THERE YOU CAN MAKE YOUR WAY SAFELY INTO GULFEN.

THANK YOU, MAX.

WELCOME ABOARD!

ARE YOU COMING WITH US?

I SHOULD STAY AND MAKE SURE NO ONE COMES AFTER YOU.

WE CAN MEET IN GULFEN.

THANKS, MAX.

I'LL SEE YOU SOON.

GET THEM TO FRONTERA AND DISAPPEAR.

DON'T STOP FOR ANYONE, UNDERSTAND?

I KNOW WHAT I'M DOING, KID.

WE'VE GOT TROUBLE!

RETURN TO THE DOCK AND PREPARE TO BE BOARDED!

IF YOU FAIL TO COMPLY, WE WILL BE FORCED TO OPEN FIRE!

WHAT DO WE DO, CAPTAIN?

WHAT DO WE DO?!

MAX GRIFFIN,

YOU HAVE BEEN SENTENCED TO FIFTY YEARS IN THE ICE PRISON OF KORTHAN FOR AIDING IN THE ESCAPE OF WAR PRISONERS.

YOU WILL ALSO FACE TRIAL IN PRISON FOR YOUR ACTIONS LEADING TO THE DEATHS OF FOUR SOLDIERS.

BEFORE WE SEND YOU OFF, DO YOU HAVE ANY LAST WORDS?

YOU WILL ALL REGRET THIS.

FIFTY YEARS LATER

HAVE YOU BEEN SITTING THERE ALL NIGHT, LOGI?

THE KING ASKED ME TO KEEP AN EYE ON YOU.

THE SUN ISN'T UP YET.

GATHER THE TROOPS.

WE START EARLY TODAY.

THE KING IS WRONG TO PUT HIS TRUST IN A TRAITOR.

EVEN IF HE IS A STONE-KEEPER.

PRINCE TRELLIS MAY HAVE BEEN A WEAKLING, BUT HE REMAINED LOYAL TO THE ELVES.

LOYAL?!

OOF!

YOUR PRINCE DESERTED AND BETRAYED ALL OF YOU!!!

WE BOTH KNOW THAT ISN'T WHAT REALLY HAPPENED, TRAITOR.

YAAGH!

HUF HUF

IF ANYONE ELSE HAS SOMETHING TO SAY TO ME, SPEAK NOW.

OTHERWISE, YOU CAN TAKE YOUR COMPLAINTS DIRECTLY TO THE KING.

MY LOYALTY LIES WITH THE NATION OF ELVES.

QUESTION ME, AND I WILL ANSWER YOU WITH THE EDGE OF MY SWORD.

WHAT ARE WE GOING TO DO, CAPTAIN?

WHAT ANY GOOD SOLDIER IS SUPPOSED TO DO!

WE STAND OUR GROUND!

BUT WE'RE OUTNUMBERED!

WE'RE HERE TO SPEAK WITH ONE OF YOUR PRISONERS.

LET US IN AND THERE WILL BE NO TROUBLE.

OUR PRISONERS DO NOT RECEIVE VISITORS!

I'M GOING TO GIVE YOU A CHOICE.

YOU CAN PLAY NICE AND OPEN THE DOOR--

FWEEEE

-- OR YOU CAN DIE,

AND I WILL DO IT MYSELF.

ERGH!

HELLO, OLD FRIEND.

KRNK KRNK

YOUR MAJESTY.

WELCOME TO THE ICE PRISON OF KORTHAN.

TELL ME ABOUT THE PRISONER.

HIS NAME IS CHRONOS, A MOUNTAIN GIANT. ONE OF THE LAST OF HIS KIND.

THOOM!

YOU KEPT YOUR PROMISE.

I'M GOING TO NEED YOU TO BE BETTER THAN THIS.

OR ELSE WE WON'T STAND A CHANCE AGAINST THE KING.

DON'T WORRY.

I CAN TAKE CARE OF MYSELF.

IT'S NOT YOU I'M WORRIED ABOUT.

IT'S EVERYONE ELSE WHOSE LIVES HANG IN THE BALANCE ON OUR ACTIONS.

I NEVER ASKED FOR THAT RESPONSIBILITY.

I FOUND SOMETHING I THINK YOU SHOULD SEE.

WHO ARE THESE PEOPLE, VIGO?

ARE THEY GHOSTS?

NOT QUITE.

THIS IS HOW THE COUNCIL RECORDS ITS MINUTES, AND STONEKEEPERS CAN ACCESS THE ARCHIVES.

I'VE BEEN HERE ALL NIGHT VIEWING THE COUNCIL'S FINAL MEETINGS.

IT'S BEEN INTERESTING SEEING WHAT TRANSPIRED AFTER I LEFT.

53

SILAS.

VIGO, HOW OLD ARE THESE RECORDINGS?

THE ONE YOU'RE WATCHING IS OVER FIFTY YEARS OLD.

HOW IS THAT POSSIBLE?

THAT WOULD MAKE MAX OLDER THAN MY MOM.

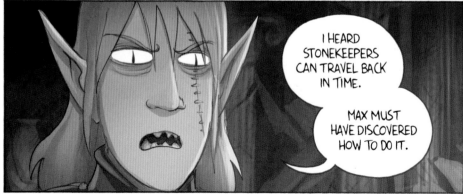

I HEARD STONEKEEPERS CAN TRAVEL BACK IN TIME.

MAX MUST HAVE DISCOVERED HOW TO DO IT.

STONEKEEPERS CANNOT TRAVEL THROUGH TIME,

BUT THEY CAN ENTER THE VOID.

THE VOID IS A DREAMSPACE BUILT OF STONEKEEPER MEMORIES.

IT IS A PLACE WHERE STONEKEEPERS CAN GO TO EXAMINE THEIR PAST AND EVEN COMMUNICATE WITH ONE ANOTHER.

SILAS CHARNON ESPOUSED THE IDEA THAT THE VOID WAS REAL, AND IT COULD ALLOW YOU TO ALTER REALITY.

BUT HIS BELIEF WAS SHADOWED BY A DESIRE TO CHANGE THE EVENTS OF HIS PAST.

SOMETIMES, PERSONAL DESIRES AND AMBITIONS CAN CLOUD THE JUDGMENT OF EVEN OUR BRIGHTEST MINDS.

BUT WHAT DID SILAS DO THAT WAS SO WRONG?

HE ENCOURAGED YOUNG STONEKEEPERS TO ENTER THE VOID.

HE DID THIS WITHOUT TRULY UNDERSTANDING THE DANGERS THEY WOULD HAVE TO FACE.

OR THE PRICE THEY MIGHT ULTIMATELY PAY.

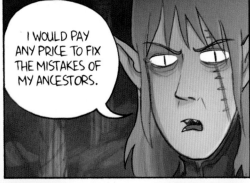

I WOULD PAY ANY PRICE TO FIX THE MISTAKES OF MY ANCESTORS.

YOU DON'T KNOW WHAT YOU ARE SAYING.

STAY OUT OF THIS.

I DO NOT KNOW HOW MAX HAS RETAINED HIS YOUTH, BUT I DID KNOW HIM ONCE.

HE WAS A STUDENT HERE AT THE ACADEMY.

WE WERE CLASSMATES.

IF WE ARE DEALING WITH THE SAME YOUNG MAN I KNEW BACK THEN --

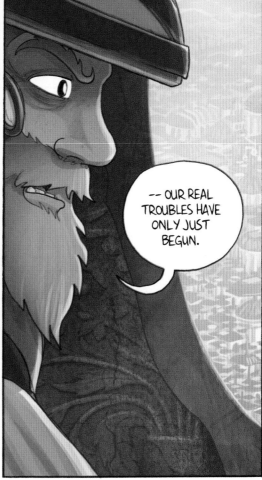

-- OUR REAL TROUBLES HAVE ONLY JUST BEGUN.

HE'LL BE WITH YOU IN A MOMENT.

READY AND WAITING FOR HIM, MA'AM!

IF YOU NEED ANYTHING, JUST TELL THE ROBOT PEOPLE TO COME LOOK FOR ME, OKAY?

I'LL BE FINE.

I LOVE YOU.

I LOVE YOU TOO, MOM.

COMMANDER NAVIN,

I AM HONORED TO BE IN YOUR PRESENCE!

I CAN HARDLY BELIEVE OUR GOOD FORTUNE!

CAN I GET YOUR AUTOGRAPH?

UH, SURE.

BUT I DON'T SEE WHY YOU'D WANT IT.

I'M NOT FAMOUS OR ANYTHING.

ALL PILOTS ARE FAMOUS HERE!

CIELIS WAS KNOWN TO HAVE THE BEST ROBOT PILOTS IN ALLEDIA.

WHAT HAPPENED TO THEM?

THEY WERE EXECUTED!

WHEN THE ELVES TOOK OVER THE GUARD, ALL OUR PILOTS WERE TOSSED OVER THE EDGE OF THE CITY.

DARK TIMES!

THE ELVES EVEN TRIED TO DISMANTLE THE COLOSSUS PROGRAM, BUT WE WERE ABLE TO SAVE A FEW UNITS BY SMUGGLING PARTS DOWN INTO THE MINES.

WE'VE BEEN REBUILDING EVER SINCE.

WHAT A MARVELOUS TURN OF EVENTS THAT YOU ARRIVED JUST AS WE WERE GETTING READY TO REACTIVATE THE COLOSSUS!

YOU WERE SIMPLY DESTINED TO BE HERE!

AND NOW THE FATE OF OUR WORLD RESTS ON YOUR SHOULDERS!

HA HA!

THESE PEOPLE ARE CRAZY.

HEY, BILL! THE PILOTS HAVE ARRIVED!

GOOD! WE ARE IN NEED OF FRESH MEAT FOR THE WAR EFFORT! NAMES, PLEASE.

MY NAME IS NAVIN. AND THIS IS COGSLEY.

THEY'RE SHRIMPY, BUT THEY'LL DO.

EVERYTHING HERE LOOKS FAMILIAR.

THAT'S NO ACCIDENT.

SILAS AND I DESIGNED HIS HOUSE TO EMULATE THE COLOSSUS.

SO YOU KNOW THESE CONTROLS, BUT THEY'RE MORE RESPONSIVE.

AND THIS MECH, UNLIKE THE CHARNON HOUSE, WAS BUILT FOR BATTLE.

LET'S SEE WHAT YOU CAN DO WITH THE REAL THING.

YOU WANT TO HEAR SOMETHING FUNNY, COGSLEY?

I MAY STILL BE PRETTY YOUNG,

AND I KNOW THERE'S A LOT LEFT FOR ME TO LEARN...

BUT I THINK THIS IS IT.

I THINK THIS IS WHAT I WAS MEANT TO DO WITH MY LIFE.

THAT WASN'T FUNNY AT ALL.

BY THE WAY,

DID YOU NOTICE THIS?

WE HAVE A THIRD SEAT.

ARE YOU NAVIN HAYES?

YES. THAT'S ME.

MY NAME IS ALYSON HUNTER.

I'LL BE JOINING YOU IN THE NEW COLOSSUS PILOT PROGRAM.

HOW WAS I CHOSEN TO BE A PART OF THIS?

HONESTLY, YOU'RE THE ONLY ONE HERE WHO HAS BEEN TO BATTLE.

THE REST OF US HAVE ONLY TRAINED ON A SIMULATOR.

WELL, THAT'S KIND OF HOW I GOT STARTED, TOO.

HEY.

THAT'S MY SISTER.

YOUR SISTER AND VIGO LIGHT ARE WHAT REMAINS OF THE GUARDIAN COUNCIL.

SHE WILL NEED TO GUIDE US ALL INTO BATTLE.

IT'S A HEAVY BURDEN FOR SOMEONE HER AGE.

OUR JOB WILL BE TO PROVIDE HER WITH SUPPORT FROM THE CIELIS GUARD.

IS THIS THE YOUNG COMMANDER?

NAVIN, THIS IS MY DAD, CAPTAIN TRISTAN HUNTER.

NICE TO MEET YOU, SON.

I HEARD YOU HAD SOME EXPERIENCE OUT IN THE FIELD.

WE'RE GOING TO NEED EVERY OUNCE OF IT HERE.

I'M READY TO HELP IN ANY WAY I CAN.

THE CITY OF FRONTERA...

... IT'S GONE. THEY LEFT NOTHING BEHIND.

AND IT APPEARS MAX IS LEADING THEM.

THEIR NEXT MOVE WILL BE TO TAKE THE CITY OF LUCIEN.

LUCIEN'S ARMY IS FORMIDABLE, BUT THEY WILL BE OVERCOME.

IT WILL SIMPLY BE A MATTER OF TIME BEFORE THEY FALL.

THEN WE NEED TO SHOW THEM THAT THE GUARDIAN COUNCIL HAS RETURNED.

BUT YOU'VE SEEN THE STATE OF THINGS HERE.

WE ARE NOT READY.

WE'LL NEVER BE READY.

AND IF WE CHOOSE TO WAIT, WE'LL MISS OUR CHANCE TO MAKE A DIFFERENCE.

WE WON'T BE ABLE TO DO THIS ALONE...

...SO WE NEED TO HELP WHOEVER IS LEFT TO FIGHT BACK.

THE LEAST WE CAN DO IS GIVE THEM HOPE.

DO YOU KNOW WHAT THIS MEANS, RICO?

THAT WE'RE GOING TO WAR?

IT MEANS WE'RE GOING HOME.

AND PEOPLE WILL KNOW THAT CIELIS REALLY DOES EXIST!

I CAN'T WAIT TO SEE THE LOOK ON EVERYONE'S FACES!

THEY'LL NEVER DOUBT ME AGAIN!

I THINK THAT SHOULD BE THE LEAST OF OUR CONCERNS RIGHT NOW, ENZO.

BROTHER, TELL ME MORE ABOUT HOW TO ACCESS EVENTS OF THE PAST.

THERE MUST BE A WAY I CAN LEARN TO DO THIS.

MASTERING THIS ABILITY WILL TAKE MANY YEARS, TRELLIS.

AND IT IS MUCH TOO DANGEROUS.

LISTEN TO THE OTHERS AND HEED THEIR WARNING.

STAY AWAY FROM SUCH DARK MAGIC.

WHY SHOULD I LISTEN TO THEM...

...WHEN THEY DON'T LISTEN TO ME?

THE SOLDIERS OF THE GUARD ARE ALL SO YOUNG. ARE YOU SURE THEY'RE READY FOR THIS FIGHT?

WE ALL HAVE TO START SOMEWHERE.

WELCOME ABOARD, YOUR HIGHNESS!

ENZO!

DON'T CALL ME THAT!

I'M GLAD TO SEE YOU GUYS.

WOULDN'T MISS THIS FOR THE WORLD!

NOT EVERY DAY YOU GET ASKED TO ESCORT THE GUARDIAN COUNCIL!

NOW, WHERE'S YOUR LITTLE BROTHER?

NAVIN'S FLYING WITH THE OTHER COLOSSUS PILOTS.

IT WILL GIVE THEM SOME TIME TO GET ACQUAINTED.

COLOSSUS PILOT! WELL, WHADDYA KNOW.

THE LITTLE RUNT'S GRADUATED TO THE BIG TIME.

HE'S ALL GROWN-UP!

DO YOU WANT ME TO HOLD ON TO DAGNO?

I CAN KEEP HIM WITH ME IN THE CABIN.

THAT'S OKAY.

HE WON'T WANT TO LEAVE HIS MAMA'S SIDE.

LOOKS LIKE WE'RE FLYING CARGO CLASS!

STAY SAFE, COGSLEY.

SEE YOU IN LUCIEN, CHIEF!

KEEP MOVING AND FIND AN OPEN SEAT.

TRELLIS, AT LEAST LET THE OTHERS KNOW.

I REALLY FEEL THAT YOU SHOULDN'T DO THIS.

AND WHY NOT, BROTHER?

DO YOU NOT WANT TO FIX OUR PAST?

WE NEED TO UNDERSTAND IT BEFORE WE CAN REPAIR IT.

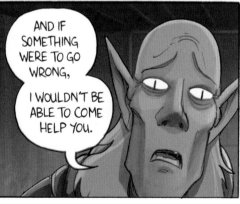

AND IF SOMETHING WERE TO GO WRONG,

I WOULDN'T BE ABLE TO COME HELP YOU.

HAS YOUR DAD ALWAYS PUT SO MUCH TRUST IN YOU?

YEAH.

I GUESS HE HAS.

IT MUST BE NICE TO HAVE YOUR DAD CLOSE BY.

HE MAKES ME FEEL MORE CONFIDENT.

HE ALWAYS TOLD ME TO IMAGINE THE KIND OF PERSON I THOUGHT OF AS A HERO --

-- AND BE THAT PERSON.

I THINK I WANT TO BE LIKE YOUR DAD.

THIS WAS AROUND THE TIME SILAS BEGAN LECTURING ABOUT THE POSSIBILITIES OF TIME TRAVEL USING THE STONES.

I SHOULD HAVE REALIZED THAT DAVID WAS BECOMING MORE INTERESTED IN THE IDEA THAN THE OTHER STUDENTS.

HE SAW IT AS AN OPPORTUNITY TO CORRECT WHAT HE FELT WAS A MISTAKE -- HE WANTED TO BRING HIS MOTHER BACK.

USING HIS POWERS, DAVID ATTEMPTED TO TRAVEL BACK TO SAVE HIS MOTHER.

BUT HE ONLY WENT INTO A DEEP SLEEP, AND DID NOT WAKE FOR DAYS.

I SAT AT HIS BEDSIDE WHILE HE SPOKE TO SOMEONE IN HIS SLEEP.

WHEN HE FINALLY OPENED HIS EYES, HE LOOKED TERRIFIED.

THEN HE WAS GONE.

SOON AFTER THAT, THE STONE RETURNED ITSELF TO ME.

WHO WAS HE TALKING TO?

I ASSUMED DAVID BELIEVED HE WAS TALKING TO HIS MOTHER.

BUT HE SPOKE ABOUT THINGS HE NEVER WOULD HAVE WITH HER.

THAT'S WHEN I REALIZED HE WAS SPEAKING TO THE STONE.

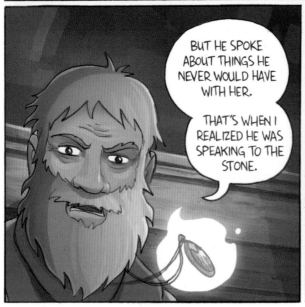

I WISHED HE FELT HE COULD TALK TO ME INSTEAD OF TURNING TO HIS IMAGINARY FRIENDS FOR HELP.

THAT'S NO WYVERN.

BOOM!

I'LL DO WHAT I CAN TO SLOW THEM DOWN.

GO GET TRELLIS.

GO NOW!

TRELLIS!

EMILY, I'M SORRY.

WHAT HAPPENED HERE?

I TRIED TO STOP HIM, BUT HE JUST WOULDN'T LISTEN.

WE NEED TO WAKE HIM UP, LUGER.

I -- CAN'T. NOT ANY- MORE.

BUT YOU -- -- YOU CAN.

HEY, CHIEF!

DON'T LEAVE US STRANDED HERE, OKAY?

WE STILL HAVE A LOT OF WORK TO DO!

I'LL BE RIGHT BACK, COGSLEY.

NAVIN, TEST THE WINGS.

THESE SILVERHAWKS HAVEN'T BEEN FLOWN IN A WHILE.

DROP ON MY MARK!

VRRRRRNN

THREE...

TWO...

...ONE!!

KCHUNG!

KCHUNG!

AAGH!

ALL OF MY TARGETS IN ONE PLACE.

WHAT KIND OF STRATEGY IS THIS?!

I HONESTLY EXPECTED MORE FROM THE BOTH OF YOU.

HE CAN'T TAKE US BOTH DOWN AT ONCE.

HE WILL HAVE TO CHOOSE.

READY WHEN YOU ARE, VIGO.

WHY ARE YOU FOLLOWING ME?

MY BROTHER TOLD ME NOT TO TALK WITH YOU.

YOU'LL WANT TO SPEAK WITH UNCLE VIRGIL.

HE'S THE ONE WHO FOUND YOU AND MENDED YOUR ARM.

HIS HOUSE IS ON THE OTHER SIDE OF THE POND.

YOU WON'T HAVE TO KNOCK.

HE IS ALREADY EXPECTING YOU.

LET ME GET YOU A SHIRT.

YOU MUST BE FREEZING.

I LOOKED UP AND SAW YOU FALL OUT OF THE SKY.

IT'S A TRUE MIRACLE THAT YOU WERE ABLE TO SURVIVE.

I THOUGHT YOU DIED.

WHERE IS EVERYONE?

POOR BOY, YOU MUST BE DELIRIOUS.

WHEN YOU FELL, YOU WERE QUITE ALONE.

HERE, TRY THIS ON.

MY FATHER'S ROBE.

HE WAS THE VILLAGE HEALER, A DOCTOR.

WOULD YOU LIKE TO HEAR A FUNNY STORY ABOUT HIM?

NO, THANKS.

I SHOULD REALLY BE GOING.

BUT WHERE ARE YOU GOING TO GO?

I HAVE TO GO AND FIND MY FRIENDS. THEY NEED MY HELP.

I SWEAR NO ONE WAS WITH YOU.

I STILL NEED TO SEE FOR MYSELF.

THANK YOU... FOR EVERYTHING.

TRELLIS!

LUGER?

WHAT DID I TELL YOU, TRELLIS?

FSK!

PEOPLE WILL COME AND ASK QUESTIONS ABOUT DAD.

YOU MUST NOT TALK TO THEM.

DON'T WORRY, LUGER.

I WASN'T TALKING WITH HIM.

HE WASN'T ASKING ABOUT DAD, ANYWAY.

WHO ARE YOU?

WE KNOW EVERYBODY ON THIS ISLAND.

AND I HAVE NEVER SEEN YOU HERE BEFORE.

STAY AWAY FROM UNCLE VIRGIL.

FATHER WILL DEAL WITH HIM LATER.

DON'T MIND MY NEPHEW LUGER.

HE'S UNDER A LOT OF PRESSURE NOW THAT HIS FATHER IS THE KING.

WHY ARE YOU HELPING ME?

SOMETHING TELLS ME THAT IT'S MY DUTY TO HELP.

AND UNLIKE MANY OF THE ELVES ON THIS ISLAND,

I HAVE A VERY GOOD SENSE OF WHO I NEED TO TRUST.

THIS LIBRARY WAS BUILT TO HONOR THAT TRADITION.

THE BOOKS CONTAINED WITHIN THESE WALLS DOCUMENT THE MANY LIVES WHO HAVE DEDICATED THEMSELVES TO FURTHERING THE ADVANCEMENT OF ELFKIND.

IT IS HOW WE HAVE PROGRESSED FASTER THAN ALL OTHER SETTLERS ON ALLEDIAN SOIL.

IT'S MOST UNFORTUNATE FOR THIS CURRENT GENERATION THAT MY BROTHER IS NOT AN AVID READER OF HISTORY.

IF HE WAS, HE WOULD SEE ALL THE WARNING SIGNS.

WARNING SIGNS?

HISTORY HAS A TENDENCY TO REPEAT ITSELF.

CAN I GET ANYTHING FOR YOU, MASTER VIRGIL?

THANK YOU, LOGI.

BUT WE'D RATHER BE LEFT TO OURSELVES.

YES, OF COURSE.

HE BECAME AN ENDURING HISTORICAL FIGURE FOR TWO REASONS.

THE FIRST WAS HIS PENCHANT FOR CONFLICT THAT SENT US INTO A CIVIL WAR.

HIS RULE MARKS THE DEADLIEST PERIOD IN ELF HISTORY.

THE SECOND WAS THAT MANY PEOPLE CLAIMED HE WAS POSSESSED BY HIS STONE.

THEY SAY HE SPOKE TO IT.

DO STONES NOT HAVE VOICES?

THE STONE IS A MEDIUM, NOT A MESSENGER.

LET ME SHOW YOU SOMETHING.

OH, GOOD.

I HID THIS ONE WELL.

I SEARCHED EVERY WING IN THIS LIBRARY FOR ANOTHER MENTION OF THE VOICE, AND I CAME UP EMPTY...

...UNTIL I FOUND THIS BOOK.

THE AUTHOR IS HUMAN, AND HE BELIEVES THAT THE STONE-SHARD AMULETS WERE CREATED TO PROVIDE THE STONEKEEPERS WITH THREE THINGS:

POWER, COMMUNICATION, AND TRAVEL.

THE AMULET GRANTS ITS KEEPER THE ABILITY TO WIELD THE KINETIC ENERGY OF THE MOTHER STONE.

BUT IT ALSO GRANTS THEM THE ABILITY TO COMMUNICATE AND TO TRAVEL USING A PLANE OF EXISTENCE PARALLEL TO OUR OWN.

WHEN THEY DO, STONEKEEPERS MAY FIND THEMSELVES UNDER THE INFLUENCE OF A DARK, GOVERNING SPIRIT -- A "VOICE."

WHY DOES THIS INTEREST YOU, VIRGIL?

BECAUSE MY BROTHER SPEAKS TO HIS STONE.

AND YOU BELIEVE HE IS SPEAKING TO THIS DARK SPIRIT?

LOOK AT THIS.

THE VOICE APPEARS EVERY TIME THE ELVES ENTER A TIME OF WAR AND STRIFE.

THIS IS FOLLOWED BY 500 YEARS OF PEACE BEFORE THE CYCLE BEGINS ANEW.

MY BROTHER WAS BORN EXACTLY 500 YEARS FROM THE DEATH OF KING LEVITAS.

MAKE OF THAT WHAT YOU WILL, BUT I FIND THE PATTERNS ALARMING.

FLIP FLIP FLIP

VIRGIL--

WHERE DID YOU GET THIS?

On Stone Power by Silas Charnon

IF THE KING FINDS THIS BOOK HE WILL HAVE YOU EXECUTED!

WHY ARE YOU TRUSTING ME WITH THIS INFORMATION?!

I'M TRUSTING YOU BECAUSE YOU NEED TO KNOW ALL OF THIS.

YOU NEED TO TAKE THIS KNOWLEDGE BACK WITH YOU.

YOU KNOW WHO I AM?

I RAISED YOU, TRELLIS.

I WOULD RECOGNIZE YOU NO MATTER HOW OLD OR YOUNG YOU WERE.

I CAME BACK TO TRY AND FIX THINGS.

IT'S BETTER THAT YOU FOCUS ON DOING WHAT'S RIGHT FOR THE FUTURE.

142

SHHHAAH

WHAT WAS THAT?

THE VOICE.

HE'S GOING TO COME AFTER YOU NOW.

YOU BETTER LEAVE.

HOW DO I GET BACK?

YOU ARRIVED IN THE WILLOW GROVE ON THAT BANK.

TAKE THE BOAT BACK TO THAT SPOT.

DRIP          DRIP

EMILY?

GET UP, TRELLIS!

HOW DID YOU FIND ME?

HOW DID YOU KNOW WHERE I WOULD BE IN THE PAST?

WE'RE NOT IN THE PAST, TRELLIS.

WE'RE IN YOUR MEMORIES!

AND I NEED YOU TO WAKE UP FROM THIS DREAM!

A DREAM?

EMILY.

EMILY,
WAKE UP.

I KNOW
HOW I CAN
HELP NOW.

THANK YOU FOR COMING TO GET ME.

EMILY WOKE YOU FROM THE VOID?

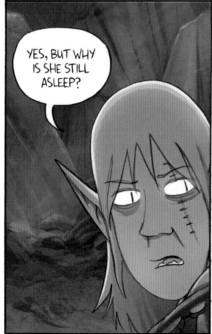

YES, BUT WHY IS SHE STILL ASLEEP?

SHE MUST STILL BE INSIDE.

HER BREATHING SEEMS REGULAR.

SHE'S IN CONTROL.

THAT MEANS SHE'S STILL ALIVE.

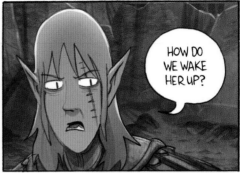

HOW DO WE WAKE HER UP?

YOU'RE THE REASON SHE'S IN THERE.

SO YOU'RE GOING BACK THERE TO GET HER OUT.

AND HOW DO I GET US BOTH BACK SAFELY?

WE WOULD NOT BE STANDING HERE IF YOU DIDN'T KNOW WHAT TO DO, TRELLIS.

ANYTHING YOU DO OUT HERE YOU WILL BE ABLE TO DO IN THE VOID.

LIKEWISE, IF YOU DIE IN THE VOID, YOU WILL DIE OUT HERE.

STAY AWAY FROM MALEVOLENT SPIRITS.

THE VOID IS, AFTER ALL, RULED BY THEM.

I'LL STAND WATCH AND KEEP YOU BOTH SAFE.

IF YOU DO NOT RETURN IN TEN MINUTES, OR IF I SEE YOU PANIC, I WILL COME AND FIND YOU, UNDERSTAND?

YOU'RE NOT GIVING ME MUCH TIME, OLD MAN.

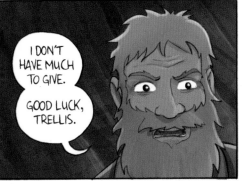

I DON'T HAVE MUCH TO GIVE.

GOOD LUCK, TRELLIS.

WHERE ARE WE?

WE'RE NEAR THE ICE PRISON OF KORTHAN.

IS THIS YOUR MEMORY?

NO.

LOOK.

MAX.

HE MUST BE DREAMING ABOUT THIS NEARBY.

I ENTERED EASILY, SO HE'S ALSO WEAK.

I'M HERE TO BRING YOU BACK.

WE SHOULD GO BEFORE--

WAIT.

YOUR TIME IS RUNNING OUT, MAX.

IF YOU GIVE UP, LAYRA WILL HAVE DIED FOR NOTHING.

KOF! KOF!

IF YOU DIE, YOU WILL LET THEM WIN.

GIVE ME CONTROL AND WE CAN MAKE THEM PAY.

I... ...AM...

...YOURS...

THANK
YOU.

SHK!

I HAVE NEVER TRUSTED HIM, BUT HE HELPED ME.

THE VOICE IS WHAT BROUGHT ME HERE.

THE VOICE BROUGHT ALL OF US HERE.

HE IS THE ONE WHO HAS TAKEN CONTROL OF MY FATHER.

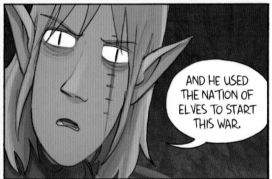

AND HE USED THE NATION OF ELVES TO START THIS WAR.

MY ANCESTORS WERE NEVER TO BLAME FOR THIS.

I WAS WRONG.

TRELLIS--

IF WE WORK TOGETHER, WE'LL STOP HIM.

WHAT IF THAT'S PART OF HIS PLAN?

THERE THEY ARE, NAVIN!

EM!

I THOUGHT YOU WERE GONE.

I WOULD NEVER LET THAT HAPPEN TO YOU.

YOU FELLAS GOT OUT OKAY?

WE'RE A LITTLE BANGED UP BUT WE'RE STILL IN BUSINESS!

PUTTING IN THIS SPARE ENGINE HAS ALREADY PAID OFF!

WHAT HAPPENED TO THE REST OF THE CONVOY?

WHEN YOU FELL, THE ATTACK SUBSIDED.

THE BEAST FOLLOWED YOU INTO THE CLOUDS.

THEN WE BETTER GET MOVING BEFORE IT COMES BACK.

ARE YOU OKAY, ALY?!

THE BATTLE IS MOVING TO THE GROUND!

I'M FINE, DAD.

IT'S ALL CLEAR DOWN HERE.

WE FOUND THE GUARDIAN COUNCIL AND ARE HEADING BACK TO YOU.

WE COULD USE AN ESCORT BACK TO THE SHIP.

I'LL SEND TWO SILVERHAWKS TO COVER YOU. JUST FLY SAFE.

THANKS FOR COMING BACK TO GET ME.

LET'S JUST SAY WE'RE EVEN.

182

NNGHH...

STAND UP, MAX.

YOU HAVE MORE WORK TO DO.

I... I CAN'T MOVE...

I THINK... ...MY BONES... ...ARE BROKEN.

AGH!

SH-KRIK!

SH-KRAK!!

PLEASE, STOP!

LAYRA...

I'M SO...
...SORRY,
LAYRA.

PLEASE...

...PLEASE...
...FORGIVE ME.

SPLISH!

END OF BOOK FIVE

CREATED AT

# BOLT CITY
## P R O D U C T I O N S
### IN ALHAMBRA, CALIFORNIA

WRITTEN AND ILLUSTRATED BY
## KAZU KIBUISHI

LEAD PRODUCTION ARTIST
## JASON CAFFOE

COLORS & BACKGROUND
### JASON CAFFOE
### ZANE YARBROUGH
### CHRYSTIN GARLAND
### KAZU KIBUISHI

PAGE FLATTING
### MARY CAGLE
### KELLY MCCLELLAN
### STUART LIVINGSTON
### DENVER JACKSON
### MEGAN BRENNAN
### JON CHUAN JU LEE

SPECIAL THANKS

Gordon & Lydia & Ellie Luk, Amy & Juni Kim Kibuishi, Judy Hansen, David Saylor, Phil Falco, Cassandra Pelham, Ben Zhu & the Gallery Nucleus crew, Nick & Melissa Harris, Nancy Caffoe, the Flight artists, Tao & Taka & Tyler Kibuishi, Tim Ganter, Rachel Ormiston, Khang Le & Adhesive Games, June & Masa & Julie & Emi Kibuishi, Sheila Marie Everett, Lizette Serrano, Bess Braswell, Whitney Steller, Lori Benton, and Ellie Berger.

And the biggest thanks of all to the librarians, booksellers, parents, and readers who have supported us all these years. You mean the world to us.

# ABOUT THE AUTHOR

Kazu Kibuishi is the creator of the #1 *New York Times* bestselling Amulet series. *Amulet, Book One: The Stonekeeper* was an ALA Best Book for Young Adults and a Children's Choice Book Award finalist. He is also the creator of *Copper*, a collection of his popular webcomic that features an adventuresome boy-and-dog pair. Kazu also illustrated the covers of the 15th anniversary paperback editions of the Harry Potter series written by J. K. Rowling. He lives and works in Seattle, Washington, with his wife, Amy Kim Kibuishi, and their children.

Visit Kazu online at www.boltcity.com.

## ALSO BY KAZU KIBUISHI

BOOK ONE
**THE STONEKEEPER**

BOOK TWO
**THE STONEKEEPER'S CURSE**

BOOK THREE
**THE CLOUD SEARCHERS**

BOOK FOUR
**THE LAST COUNCIL**

BOOK FIVE
**PRINCE OF THE ELVES**

BOOK SIX
**ESCAPE FROM LUCIEN**